ALICE'S WORLD RECORD

By the same author:

Alice's Birthday Pig
Alice's Shooting Star
Circle of Doom
Sabine

ALICE'S WORLD RECORD

TIM KENNEMORE

Illustrated by Mike Spoor

Andersen Press • London

For Ruth

This edition published in 2006 by
Andersen Press Limited,
20 Vauxhall Bridge Road, London SW1V 2SA
www.andersenpress.co.uk

Reprinted 2007

Text © Tim Kennemore, 1996, 2006
Illustrations © Mike Spoor, 2006

The rights of Tim Kennemore and Mike Spoor to be
identified as the author and illustrator of this work have been
asserted by them in accordance with the Copyright, Designs
and Patents Act, 1988.

British Library Cataloguing in Publication Data available
ISBN 978 1 84270 238 3

Phototypeset by Intype Libra Ltd
Printed in the UK by CPI Bookmarque, Croydon, CR0 4TD

Contents

1

Polly Penguin Done It

One Monday, as Alice Singer's family were sitting down to tea, there came the most dreadful noise from the front room.

The noise sounded like this:

'OHNOEEEAARRGGH!ARGLE!YARG! WHERE'SROSIEI'MGONNAKILLHERSCL URBLEAARGHYURGGHHH!'

It was the sound of Alice's brother Oliver, losing his temper.

Everyone looked at Alice's little sister Rosie.

'Polly Penguin done it,' said Rosie.

Oliver stormed into the kitchen waving what looked like a rather large jam sandwich.

'Look what she's done!' he shouted.

Everyone looked.

'She's spread strawberry jam all over my school library book! All over *Chess Openings for Improving Players Part One*!'

'Polly Penguin done it,' said Rosie, sadly. Rosie was too young and too terrible to have a real pet of her own. Instead she had Polly Penguin. Polly Penguin, who had once been Alice's favourite soft toy, lived in a shoebox out on the patio with Alice's guinea pig Aminal and Oliver's rabbit Peter. Whenever Rosie was caught doing something naughty she would say 'Polly Penguin done it.'

The damage done by Polly Penguin to the Singers' house was almost unbelievable for one small cuddly toy. Polly Penguin's favourite game was to unwind a whole roll of toilet paper from the cardboard in the middle, and wrap it all around the house. Polly Penguin liked to put people's shoes in the washing machine, with a bar of soap, and to switch the machine on. Only last week Polly Penguin had been so very, very

bad as to take a large frozen chicken, which was thawing in the kitchen, and to bury it in a hole in the back garden. There had been a lot of trouble about that.

And now this.

'Look what you've done!' screamed Oliver. 'I'll get into trouble, and it's the Chess Tournament tomorrow and it's the most important day of my life! I hate you! I don't want you for my sister! I want to go and live with Grandma Fox in Bristol!'

Grandma Fox was Mum's mum. She was Oliver's favourite grandparent and he was her favourite grandchild. They both believed in doing things properly, keeping things tidy, and making sure that small, naughty children were looked after by other people and kept well out of their way, preferably locked up securely in a cage.

'Polly Penguin done it,' said Rosie, patiently.

Mum said that as Rosie wasn't looking after Polly Penguin properly, from now on Rosie would be punished for all the things Polly Penguin did wrong.

Rosie looked at Oliver's strawberry chess book, thought about things for a while and said: 'Alice done it!'

'Alice *did* it!' said Oliver, who was very badly upset, but not so upset that he was going to let Rosie get away with saying things the wrong way.

'I didn't do it!' shouted Alice.

'I don't mean that you *did* it,' said Oliver, going pink in the face with crossness and with trying to explain. 'I mean Rosie mustn't say *done* when she ought to say *did*. I know that Polly Penguin did it. I mean . . .'

'Polly Penguin!' said Rosie, and looked up at her mother as if to say: 'You see what I mean? Even Oliver says Polly Penguin did it so how can you possibly blame me?'

None of this did Rosie any good and she was sent up to bed with no tea.

'Don't want beans! Don't want ice cream!' screamed Rosie as she was carried up the stairs. Mum promised Oliver she'd go in to school with him next day and explain about the library book and pay for it so he wouldn't get into trouble.

Polly Penguin was remarkably good for the rest of the evening.

2

Rainbow Dice

The next morning was the day of Oliver's School Chess Tournament. He was pale and shaky with nerves at breakfast time. He couldn't eat his cornflakes because his hand wobbled so much that they all tipped out, and the spoon rattled and chattered against his teeth.

'It's only a game, Oliver,' said Dad. 'Try and relax and enjoy yourself. That's what it's supposed to be for.'

Oliver sat and shook. His skin was as white as if someone had taken all his blood out and filled him up with milk instead.

'But what if I d . . . d . . . don't win?' he said.

'Nobody will think any the less of you,' said Dad.

'Of course they will,' said Oliver. 'They'll think I'm not such a good chess player as somebody else!'

'Does that really matter so very, very much?' said Mum. 'Being a brilliant chess player doesn't make you a better person. Most of the famous players I can think of seem to have been either horrible or mad, or both. Here, try some toast. You aren't getting anywhere with those cornflakes.'

Oliver didn't want any toast. 'You just don't understand!' he said.

Alice understood. The thing about Oliver was that he could just never bear to lose at anything. It didn't matter if it was chess or tiddlywinks. When he won he gave off a satisfied glow. He was at his nicest. He would even try to help you by telling you where you had gone wrong. But when he lost, a huge black cloud descended over him. The rest of the day would be ruined. He would say: 'It's not fair!' or 'I had a headache!' or 'I wasn't playing properly anyway!' or 'I couldn't concentrate because my foot was sore!' He had always been the same. He had probably been born that way. Alice was very glad she was different. At least she could relax and enjoy games. Oliver never relaxed. He never laughed. He never had any fun.

Of course, this made him very difficult to play games with, and hardly anyone except Rosie would play with him any more. Mum played chess with him now and then, which was safe enough because Oliver always won. But sometimes Rosie would persuade Oliver to play Rainbow Dice with her, and this was always a dreadful mistake. The trouble with Rainbow Dice was that it was entirely a game of luck. You took three rainbow dice, each with a different colour on every face, and then you had to throw the right colours to fill up your board. So being older and cleverer didn't help Oliver at all. Rosie was just as likely to win as he was, and to have Rosie beating him at anything made Oliver almost ill.

'I hate this stupid game!' he would shout,

knocking the board and all the dice across the carpet. 'I hate this family! I want to go and live with Grandma Fox in Bristol!'

Rosie thought this was great fun. 'I'm the winner!' she would say happily, collecting up all the dice and putting them neatly back into the box, for all the world as if she were a person who usually picked things up instead of being a person who nearly always threw them onto the floor. 'Oliver been naughty. I'm the winner.'

It was a strange thing, but Rosie, who had a worse temper than anyone else in the house, and probably a worse temper than anyone in the world, never minded a bit about winning and losing games. Even when Oliver won, she just said: 'I'm the winner!'

Oliver tried very hard to explain to her that she had lost. 'Look, Rosie,' he said. 'I just threw a red, which was all I needed. You still need green and yellow. I'm the winner.'

Now *this* made Rosie cross. It made her so cross that she hurled all the dice, and

the shaker and the board, at Oliver. So
whoever won, the game ended with dice
thrown all round the room and with
somebody losing their temper.

Alice never played Rainbow Dice with
them any more.

3

You Win Three Bananas

Every Tuesday after school Alice cleaned
Aminal's hutch, which was kept out on the
patio up against the kitchen wall. She chose
Tuesdays because that was the day Oliver
went to Chess Club. The good thing about
this was that it meant he wasn't there on
the patio with Alice, cleaning out Peter's
hutch, watching Alice and telling her she
wasn't doing it properly.

'You really should clean your guinea pig
on Saturdays when I do Peter Rabbit,' he
would say. 'Then there would be people
around to help you.' Oliver would never
call Aminal by his real name. He said this
was because it wasn't a proper name, but

the real reason was that he couldn't say it. It simply never came out the right way. He could only say *Animal*, which was quite wrong.

This was the reason for Aminal's name. *Aminal* was what used to come out of Alice's mouth whenever she tried to say *Animal*, and Oliver had teased and teased her about it. So when she had been given the guinea pig for her last birthday, she called him Aminal, and all of a sudden her word was right and Oliver's word, *Animal*, was wrong.

Alice liked to do things her own way, and she didn't need any help cleaning a hutch out, especially not from Oliver, who never actually helped at all. Rosie trotted outside with her. While Alice was cleaning out Aminal, Rosie would clean out Polly Penguin. Polly was supposed to live in a shoebox next to Aminal's hutch, but because she was such a particularly naughty penguin she was very rarely at home.

Alice had a large cardboard box to put Aminal in while she was getting his hutch ready. Sometimes Mum or Dad might sit

Aminal on their lap, but usually they were too busy. On the day of Oliver's Chess Tournament, Dad was home and Mum was picking Oliver up. Mum was usually the one who fetched Oliver from Chess Club, because she could play chess herself and so she could make some sense of what Oliver was telling her about pawns and queens and sacrifices and checkmates. Alice asked Dad if he'd hold Aminal, but he was much too busy making a risotto which, he said, would be the best risotto they had ever eaten in their lives.

Alice lifted Aminal carefully out of his hutch and lowered him into the box. He shivered and looked up at her sadly, his nose twitching. He had never liked the box. There weren't any windows and he couldn't see anything except sky. Rosie dropped Polly Penguin into the box with Aminal. Aminal gave Polly Penguin a hopeful sort of sniff. Rosie used Aminal's bedding in Polly Penguin's shoe box, and Polly Penguin was sometimes put in Aminal's hutch to visit. This meant that Polly Penguin was starting to have the same fluffy sawdusty smell as Aminal, and for a few wonderful moments it seemed to Aminal that Polly Penguin might be another guinea pig, come to play.

Alice changed all Aminal's old smelly bedding, and gave him fresh food and water. Then she went indoors to fetch a special present she had bought him with fifty pence of her pocket money. A sheet of butterfly stickers.

'I want that,' said Rosie.

Alice growled at her. She peeled all the stickers off one by one and stuck them carefully to the inside of Aminal's hutch. There were fifteen stickers altogether. By the time she had finished there were butterflies all over the walls, and two on the ceiling. Alice thought it looked wonderful. She lifted Aminal out of the cardboard box and put him back in his newly decorated hutch. Aminal looked amazed at the sight of the butterflies.

'Polly Penguin wants that,' said Rosie dangerously.

'There's all the white bits left for Polly

Penguin,' said Alice. 'Look.' She picked up the sticker page and began to peel off the outside. It all came off in one piece; a rectangle of white sticky paper with butterfly shaped holes in it. Rosie looked at this for a while, then took it and began to tear it into pieces, which she stuck on Polly Penguin's shoe box. Alice breathed a sigh of relief.

Suddenly there was the sound of the front door slamming and of Oliver running into the kitchen.

'I won!' he shouted. 'I won the Chess Tournament!'

'Wonderful!' said Dad.

'I've got a trophy!' said Oliver.

'Wonderful!' said Dad. 'Mind my risotto. It's not as if it were any old risotto. Tender baby button mushrooms, sliced into razor-thin slivers and delicately fried in butter . . .'

Oliver rushed outside to the patio to show Alice and Rosie.

'Look!' he said. 'I won!' He was waving something wildly around in the air.

'Can I see?' asked Alice.

Oliver gave her the trophy to look at. It was really very interesting. It was shaped like a silver goblet, but with handles on both sides, and where the handles joined the cup the silver had been made into the shape of a chess king and queen. The trophy had a wooden base which was patterned on top with pale and dark brown squares like a chess board. Alice couldn't imagine ever being clever enough to win such a glorious thing. For a moment she felt quite proud to have Oliver for a brother. This wasn't something she felt very often.

Rosie looked at the trophy and at Oliver. 'Don't want that stupid shiny eggcup!' she shouted, before Oliver had a chance to tell her she couldn't have it.

Mum came out to join them on the patio. 'What about this, then?' she said. 'A trophy! I think this deserves a treat, Oliver, though for heaven's sake don't ask for chicken legs for tea, because your father's cooking risotto and we all have to pretend it's the best risotto there's ever been in the world.'

'I heard that!' shouted Dad from inside.

'All I want is to play chess!' said Oliver. 'I can't think of anything else but chess. Let's have a game, Mum.'

'But you always win!' said Mum.

This was not a problem for Oliver.

'All right then,' said Mum. 'Let me just say hello to Animal, I mean' – she drew a deep breath – '*Aminal.*'

'Well done,' said Alice. Mum bent down and peered into the hutch.

'Goodness!' she said. 'He's had the decorators in!'

'What do you mean?' said Oliver, crouching down beside her.

'Butterflies!' said Mum. Aminal was huddled in the far corner of his hutch, still blinking with astonishment.

'Do you think he likes them?' Alice asked, nervously. For all she knew, guinea pigs were terrified of butterflies and Aminal would have nightmares for weeks.

'He doesn't look as if he does,' said Oliver.

'Oh, I think he will,' said Mum. 'I think he'll be glad of something to look at, once he gets used to them. I remember, when we had the front room decorated it took your father months to get used to it, and he's fine now. I wouldn't worry.'

Alice went indoors with them to watch the chess game. It always sounded as if it ought to be interesting – more interesting than anything else that was going on in the house, anyway. Then after a few minutes she would remember what it was really like. Alice enjoyed most games but chess was absolutely no fun at all. Mum and Oliver just sat there and stared at the board, which was just plain brown and white squares. None of them said 'Go back one square' or 'Advance to Go' or 'Collect a thousand pounds' or anything like that. There weren't any dice to roll or cards to pick up with exciting messages like 'You win three bananas from the player on your left'. And then there was Oliver. Oliver sat hunched tight, his fists clenched white, all of him screwed up into a ball of concentration. He was trying so hard he was nearly bursting. It looked like a great waste of effort because he always seemed to win quite easily. There was something about the sight of Oliver playing chess that made Alice want to rush up and down the garden, waving her arms about like a windmill and shouting complete nonsense at the top of her voice.

She couldn't imagine what would happen if Oliver lost. But, of course, he never did.

4

Possible Queues Ahead

The weekend after that was Grandma Fox's birthday. Every year they all drove down to Bristol for the day with her birthday present. Last year Rosie had drawn scribbles all over Grandma Fox's nice white hall with a sticky red felt pen. Alice had hoped that this meant that they wouldn't have to go again, but it seemed that Rosie had been forgiven.

Of course Grandpa Fox would be there as well but you never really thought of it as visiting him because he never seemed somehow to be around. He was always busy decorating something or fixing something or building something or doing secret

29

things in the garden shed. He would poke his head through the door and say hello, and he hoped they wouldn't mind if he didn't stop, because he was right in the middle of his grouting and the plaster would set. He seemed to spend more time in the garden shed than he did in the house. Alice thought this was very sensible of him. If she had to live with Grandma Fox all the time she'd want to move out to the shed as well.

When Grandpa Fox had seen what Rosie had done to the hall with the red pen he had been quite excited about it. 'I'll have to redecorate this from top to bottom now!' he said. He looked like someone who had just been given a present. Grandpa Fox had a soft spot for Rosie, and often took her off to help him in the garden.

Grandma Fox did not have a soft spot for Rosie. Grandma Fox liked Oliver best. She thought Oliver was absolutely wonderful. She thought Oliver was exactly what children ought to be like. She had twice as many photographs of Oliver as she did of

Alice or Rosie, and she always gave him much better presents. She didn't mind Alice, as long as Alice was quiet and good and didn't annoy her, but then she never took much notice of her either. Rosie she thought was the worst child in the world.

They had to leave early Saturday morning.

'Are you sure Aminal will be all right?' Alice said for the hundredth time, as Mum and Dad loaded bags into the car boot. It would be a long lonely day for Aminal, and she was sure he'd miss her, and if he got ill there would be nobody to look after him.

'Don't worry,' said Dad. 'You've filled up his water bottle and given him plenty of food. He'll be just fine. He's got Peter Rabbit for company!'

Alice didn't think much of that. Oliver's rabbit was the most boring animal she had ever known in her life. He was getting more and more like Oliver all the time. She could just imagine what it would be like for poor Aminal, with Peter Rabbit sitting there in the hutch opposite gazing over at him in a sniffy sort of way, as if to say that Aminal was making a mess with his food and he really ought to learn to eat properly. Polly Penguin would be better company, only Polly Penguin had mysteriously disappeared a couple of days ago. But there was nothing more she could do for Aminal, so she got into the car.

Alice always had to sit in the middle of the back seat, the very worst place. This was because Rosie's seat had to go next to one window, and Oliver had to sit by the other one because otherwise he got carsick. Alice had never seen Oliver be carsick, but he said this was because he always sat by the window.

Rosie could open the belt and straps of her car seat so she had to be tied in with string. 'I want Polly Penguin!' she said, while Mum tied several very tight knots.

'Absolutely not,' said Mum. It had been decided that Polly Penguin was too naughty to be allowed to go to Grandma Fox's. There was no telling what might happen if Polly Penguin was let loose on Grandma

Fox's beautiful, perfectly tidy house.

Alice slid into her place, Oliver climbed in beside her, and Mum got into the driving seat. Mum and Dad usually did half the driving each, stopping halfway to untie Rosie and take her to the loo.

'Let's play the Alphabet Game!' said Oliver to Alice.

'All right,' said Alice. She liked the Alphabet Game. What you had to do was to look out of the window and find a word starting with A, then one with B, then one with C, all the way through to Z. Alice had never in her life got to Z. She usually got stuck on Q and then fell asleep somewhere on the motorway. It was a safe game to play because Oliver always won. As Oliver was at least nine inches taller than Alice and he had a window to look out of while she was stuck in the middle, this wasn't surprising.

They both always got A very quickly because their road was called Ashton Road and the road at the end of it was called South Avenue. After that it depended which way they were going. If they were heading towards the motorway you had to try very hard to get as far on in the alphabet as you could before the motorway began, because after that there were no street names or shops and it got very difficult. There was nothing but road signs and lorries on the motorway and Oliver nearly always saw those first.

Alice was on E and Oliver was on G when Rosie suddenly said: 'Polly Penguin did hide in the car!'

There was a long silence.

'Where did Polly Penguin hide, Rosie?' asked Dad.

'Under your seat,' said Rosie, shaking her head sadly at the wickedness of Polly Penguin.

Alice bent down, scrabbled around under Dad's car seat and pulled Polly out.

'Very naughty!' said Rosie sorrowfully.

'G!' said Oliver. 'Gordon's the Chemist.'

'Rosie,' said Mum, 'if Polly Penguin does one single naughty thing at Grandma Fox's, just one, she's going in the bin!'

Alice thought this was a bit much.

'Polly Penguin used to be mine!' she said. 'You can't do that!'

'In the bin!' said Mum. Alice sighed. It was hard enough to keep out of trouble herself, and now she'd have to keep an eye on Rosie as well.

'H!' said Oliver. 'Halifax Building Society.'

Alice had to work very hard to catch up now. Luckily Oliver got stuck on K for quite a long time, and when they reached the motorway she was on P and he was on Q.

They drove on for quite a long time without anyone getting anything, and Mum and Dad began to talk about changing the rules for the really difficult letters like Q and X and Z.

'The game just gets stuck on Q every time,' said Mum. 'Perhaps we should let it count if they see it on a car number plate.'

'That would be too easy,' said Dad.

'Or perhaps it should count if you see a word with a Q in it anywhere.'

'You're too soft,' said Dad.

'X!' said Rosie.

37

'Don't be silly, Rosie,' said Oliver. 'You haven't even got an A yet.'

'X!' said Rosie, cuddling Polly Penguin. 'I got an X!'

Oliver, who had had his nose pressed up against his window watching the lorries go by in the other direction, turned round and started to explain to Rosie why she couldn't have an X. 'If you're going to play then you must play properly, Rosie. Now, what you do is . . .'

Alice yawned. She couldn't understand why Oliver didn't just ignore Rosie. She thought she might be about to go to sleep. She hadn't even got P yet, let alone Q. And then, suddenly, a large sign came into view through the front window. Oliver, who was still telling Rosie the rules, hadn't seen it. And the sign grew close enough for Alice to read it. She blinked. She could hardly believe it. The sign said:

POSSIBLE
QUEUES
AHEAD

'P and Q!' yelled Alice. 'Possible Queues!'

'Well done, Alice!' said Dad.

'What?' screamed Oliver, looking round just in time to see the sign disappear behind them in a flash. 'What did she say?'

'Possible Queues Ahead!' sang Alice. She had got Q! For the first time in her life she had got Q, and she was beating Oliver!

'It couldn't have been!' said Oliver. 'There's no such sign! I've never seen one before! You didn't see it, did you, Dad?'

'Afraid so,' said Dad.

'But it's not fair!' shouted Oliver. 'I wasn't looking because I had to tell Rosie how to play properly. One of you should have told her!'

'I didn't really think it mattered,' said Mum. 'Calm down, Oliver. If you scream into my ear like that again I'll have an accident.'

'But it's not *fair*,' moaned Oliver. 'I would have seen it first!'

'W!' said Rosie, with a wicked glint in her eye. Oliver screwed up his fists and pressed them up against his eyes and went very quiet. And so he didn't see what Alice could see: an enormous, slow, green lorry up ahead in the distance. They were catching it up fast. Alice squeezed a sideways glance at Oliver out of the corner of her eye. He still wasn't looking. And Alice could see that there were several words on the back of the lorry. Whatever they were, if they were any use at all, Alice would get them.

And then they were close enough to read the words.

It couldn't be true, could it? Could it? Could it possibly? She checked and double-checked. She triple-checked. It was true. This was what it said on the back of the lorry:

LONG VEHICLE
ROUTINE SKID
TESTING UNDER
WAY

'R, S, T, U, V and W!' said Alice.
Mum and Dad both cheered.
'I think that's the world record!' said
Mum. 'I've never seen anything like it!'
'That definitely wins a prize!' said Dad.
From Alice's right there came the sound
of Oliver bursting into tears.
The rest of the journey was no fun at all.

5

Grandma and Grandpa Fox

Twenty minutes later, when they stopped at a service station to untie Rosie and change drivers, Oliver refused to get out of the car. He wouldn't talk to anybody. He just sat scrunched up in the corner of the back seat and didn't move.

'Come along, old man,' said Dad.

Oliver buried his head in his hands and made a snivelling noise.

'Move!' said Dad. 'Out!'

Nothing happened.

'Wet myself in a minute,' said Rosie, wriggling and squirming.

'All right, then, we'll leave you here,' said Dad to Oliver.

Mum sighed. 'We can't really leave him on his own,' she said. 'I'll stay and talk to him. Alice, you go with your father and take Rosie into the loo.'

Alice groaned. Taking Rosie to a public toilet was no fun at all. It was a nightmare. These were just some of the things Rosie had done so far in public toilets:

1. Dropped her new furry mittens into the toilet.
2. Used a whole packet of toilet paper, which caused a very nasty flood.
3. Stolen a handbag from the woman in the next toilet by pulling it through by the strap. The police were very understanding but Alice had nearly died of shame.

So you had to go in with her and watch her with eyes in the back of your head, and there was never enough room, and Rosie would stick her legs straight out in front and kick you in the stomach. And then she would insist on flushing the toilet herself even if you had to lift her up to reach it. And then you had to lift her up again to reach the sink so that she could wash her hands, and you didn't have a free hand to turn the taps on for her, and you never knew how the taps were going to work anyway, and there would always be a horrible mess with the soap. And everyone else would be *watching* you. And then you would have to stand around waiting for the automatic hand drier to turn itself off because Rosie would never leave until it had finished. Her arms weren't long enough to reach that either, so she always ended up dripping wet anyway, and you had to hold her hand to get her out so you ended up damp yourself.

'Sorry about that, Alice,' said Dad, as Alice and Rosie came out from the women's toilets, Alice holding on grimly, Rosie struggling to escape.

'That was *terrible*,' said Alice. She could have *killed* Oliver. They should have *made* him get out of the car.

'Let's go to the shop and find something

for your prize,' said Dad, grabbing Rosie and lifting her up onto his shoulders.

Alice cheered up at that. She had almost forgotten about the prize. It didn't seem real, somehow. She still could hardly believe that she had actually beaten Oliver at anything, let alone broken the world record. She wandered round in a daze. There were puzzles and crayons and magazines and books and sweets, but while she would have *quite* liked any of these things there was nothing that seemed special enough for this prize. She explained this to Dad and he understood perfectly.

'We'll save it for when you see something special enough,' he said.

'You won't forget, will you?' It might take weeks before something special turned up. It might take months.

'I'll give you a written promise,' said Dad. He took some paper and a pen from his pocket, wrote something down, tore it off and gave it to Alice. It said: 'I owe Alice one special thing for breaking the world record at the Alphabet Game.'

This seemed excellent to Alice.

But back in the car things hadn't improved at all.

'Oliver wasn't in the mood for talking,' said Mum. 'I gave up trying, after a while.'

'I'm sure he'll cheer up when we get to Grandma Fox's,' said Dad, climbing into the driver's seat. 'He always does.'

Oliver sniffed. Dad started the car and pulled out of the service station back on to the motorway.

Just before they got to Grandma Fox's house they drove past something exciting. There were brightly coloured vans and lorries parked in a field, and all around were roundabouts, stalls and swingboat rides, with a huge big wheel in the middle circling up into the sky. A fairground!

'Look!' squeaked Alice. 'The fair! Can we go? Please?'

'Sorry, Alice,' said Mum. 'We're only here for the day, and we're visiting Grandma Fox for her birthday.'

Alice sighed. Grandma Fox never seemed to like Alice particularly so you'd think she'd be glad for Alice to be at the fair out of her way. All of a sudden a vivid memory came into her head. 'That fair was here last year too!' she said. 'And we couldn't go then either!'

'It comes here every autumn,' said Mum.

'And we told Grandma Fox about it,' said Alice, still remembering, 'and she said it was dirty and rough.'

'I'm afraid so,' said Dad. They drove on past the fair and Alice turned to gaze out of the back window as it disappeared. The fair wasn't open yet, but she could almost see the flashing lights of the roundabouts as they whirled round, and hear the loud distorted magical sound of the fairground music. It made it seem a hundred times worse that they were going to Grandma Fox's.

A few minutes later they had arrived, and Dad parked the car in the road. Mum untied Rosie, who was cuddling Polly Penguin and smiling like a little angel, and they all piled out and went to ring the bell.

Except for Oliver. Oliver stayed in the

car, all cold and pale, with his arms folded tight. He hadn't spoken to anyone for an hour and a half and he didn't move.

Grandma Fox opened the door and looked at them. 'Hello, everyone!' she said. She gave Mum a kiss and smiled all around, the smile only fading as she caught sight of Rosie, who stood still and sweet and beamed up at her warmly.

'Hello, Grandma Fox!' said Rosie.

'Hello, Roseanna,' said Grandma Fox faintly. Grandma Fox was the only person in the world who called Rosie by her full name. She gazed down at Rosie as if wishing to check her for weapons before allowing her in the house. Rosie snuggled up against Mum's legs and fluttered her eyelashes and pretended to be shy. Grandma Fox looked more suspicious at this than if Rosie had charged at her full-tilt waving a thick red felt pen.

Then Grandma Fox said: 'Where's Oliver?'

'In the car,' said Dad.

Now he's going to get it, thought Alice.

Suddenly it seemed that this was the moment she'd been waiting for all her life. At last Grandma Fox, who thought that Oliver was perfect and had never seen what he could *really* be like, was going to see him being sulky and rude. Really, really rude. Ruder than Alice had ever been in her life. And all because he'd lost a game and Alice was World Champion. Alice lost games all the time, and it seemed that she had been losing games to Oliver ever since she had been born. And she had never ever minded or complained or sulked. Alice had never been naughty like Rosie. She had always been good and quiet and polite and behaved properly, and all these years Grandma Fox had preferred Oliver anyway. Well, all that was about to change. Because Grandma Fox got absolutely *furious* about rudeness. Surely nothing would ever be the same again.

But:

'Oh, he's not been carsick?' said Grandma Fox. 'Poor old Oliver. Alice, I hope you didn't have a silly little fight over

the window seat, did you? You know Oliver
feels *so* poorly if he can't sit by a window.'
And before Alice could say a word
Grandma Fox had swept out to their car
and opened Oliver's door and was giving
him a big hug.

Oliver got out of the car. He staggered
out, holding his tummy. He looked so pale
and ill that anyone would think he *had*
been carsick.

'Come in and sit quietly and have a nice
cool drink,' said Grandma Fox. And that
was the end of that.

Alice couldn't believe it. Dad gave her
shoulder a big squeeze, as if to say he knew
what she was feeling. He pointed to her
pocket where she had hidden her secret
note from him. Alice gave a faint smile. But
the day had fallen to pieces. For a moment
she wished that the Special Thing that Dad
owed her could be that they never had to
drive to Bristol and see Grandma Fox
again. But she knew this would never
happen because she was Mum's mum and
they would always have to see her forever.

Inside, Oliver had had a drink of old-fashioned still lemonade and thought he was starting to feel a bit better. Although he still didn't feel properly well he managed to be brave enough to go out to the car and fetch in Grandma Fox's birthday present, a large pot plant in a terracotta pot holder which they'd had to wedge in with cushions in the boot so it wouldn't fall over.

'Oh, thank you, Oliver!' said Grandma Fox. 'Thank you, everybody!' she remembered to say a moment afterwards. Grandpa Fox poked his head in through the back door and said hello everybody, he hoped they'd excuse him if he didn't come in but he was turning over the vegetable garden and his boots were squelchy with mud from tip to toe.

Grandma Fox put her pot plant in the conservatory and made toasted sandwiches for lunch. Alice sat quiet and still in a corner and wondered what on earth they were going to do for the rest of the day. Grandpa Fox took his muddy boots off and pottered inside for a sandwich. This reminded Oliver to get out his chess trophy to show everyone.

'Clever lad,' said Grandpa Fox, from underneath Rosie who had climbed on his knee with Polly Penguin and was feeding him bits of toasted sandwich.

Grandma Fox took the trophy in her hands and turned it round and round. You would think she had never seen a trophy in her life before. She looked at it and then looked at Oliver and back at the trophy again as if she were about to burst. Oliver managed to force down three toasted sandwiches despite having been so very poorly. Alice looked at the clock and worked out that there were at least six hours left before they could start driving back and possibly even seven. And then there would be two and a half hours in the car, and she'd have to go straight to bed when they got back, and that would be *it*. Somehow she had expected more of a day when she had broken a world record. Somehow Oliver had managed to spoil it and he had got away with it.

6

Top of the World

Things got worse. After lunch Grandpa put Rosie's pink elephant boots on and took her and Polly Penguin back outside to do gardening. Dad went out with them to look at the vegetable garden. He was always meaning to grow vegetables himself. But somehow everything Grandpa Fox planted grew and grew, while everything Dad planted shrivelled up and died or got eaten by slugs. They had the happiest, fattest slugs in London, Dad said. All the slugs in the neighbourhood came round to their house for parties. He might as well give up and put out crisps and balloons for the slugs so they could really enjoy themselves. He

might as well put out saucers of beer to wash the lettuce down. It was hopeless.

Alice gazed bleakly out through the window at them. 'And now let me tell you what I've got planned for this afternoon,' Grandma Fox was saying. 'I know a very special shop in town where they sell chess sets. I know you've only got an old cheap one, and I thought it was time Oliver had a really nice set of his own. So I thought we'd all go into the city centre and Oliver can choose a set, as a special treat for winning his School Chess Tournament.'

'Now that's a wonderful idea,' said Mum, brightening up. Mum *loved* going shopping. 'As it happens I need some new shoes. There must be at least half a dozen shoe shops in the city centre to choose from.'

A huge gloomy blackness fell on Alice at the thought of being taken round six different shoe shops while Mum tried on shoes.

'And I need a jumper!' said Grandma Fox. 'Good. We'll set off in a quarter of an hour, then. Roseanna seems quite happy in the garden, so I think we'll leave her behind. That will mean we can do our shopping in peace. Good.'

This was absolutely desperate. Shoes! Jumpers! Chess sets! Without Rosie screaming and whingeing that she wanted to go home it could take *hours*. And it was a Saturday afternoon, and there would be millions of people pushing and shoving and trampling on Alice and knocking her over. Her mother never seemed to notice this.

Suddenly Alice had an idea. She raced out of the room and into the back garden.

'Dad!' she shouted.

Dad came over. 'What's the matter?' he said.

'Shopping!' said Alice.

'Shopping?' said Dad.

'Grandma Fox wants us all to go shopping for a chess set in the city centre!' said Alice.

'Oh dear,' said Dad.

'And they're going to buy shoes and jumpers!' said Alice.

'Not shoes and jumpers!' said Dad,

looking worried.

'They'll probably go to Marks and Spencers,' said Alice. 'Dad, I've known Mum spend a whole hour in the women's clothes section of Marks and Spencers!'

'It's not possible!' said Dad, looking seriously alarmed.

'A whole hour!' said Alice. 'And that's before she even *starts* on the shoe shops. You don't know what it's like. You never go. I've *been*.'

'Alice,' said Dad, 'this is desperate.'

'That's what I thought,' said Alice.

'We have to make a plan,' said Dad.

'I've got a plan!' said Alice.

'You have?' said Dad.

'We'll go to the fair!' said Alice.

'We'll go to the fair!' said Dad. 'Hang on a second. *What* did you just say?'

'I said we'll go to the fair!' said Alice. She pulled out the secret note from her pocket and read it out loud. '"I owe Alice one special thing for breaking the world record at the Alphabet Game." This is the special thing I want.'

'Hmm,' said Dad. 'I don't know about that. I mean . . .'

'Shoe shops!' said Alice.

'But what about Rosie and Oliver?' said Dad, shuddering at the very thought of shoe shops.

'Rosie's quite happy here with Grandpa Fox,' said Alice, pointing. 'Look.' Dad looked. It was true. Rosie was standing ankle deep in mud digging with a little spade and chattering to Grandpa Fox. From time to time Grandpa Fox said: 'Polly Penguin did *what?*' They looked completely peaceful together.

'And Oliver has to choose his chess set,' said Alice. The thought that Oliver would also have to spend hours looking at jumpers in Marks and Spencers didn't bother her one little bit. He deserved it for being such a bad loser at the Alphabet Game. He deserved it for making Mum stay with him so Alice had to take Rosie to the toilets. He . . . he just *deserved* it.

They went to the fair. Grandma Fox was horrified when they told her. 'But it's dirty and rough!' she said.

'Never mind,' said Dad. 'I'll take good care of both of us.'

Alice could see a silent scream starting to explode inside Oliver. He hated going shopping as much as she did. He was *dying* to go to the fair. But he couldn't say a word, because then Grandma Fox would be offended and he wouldn't get his chess set.

Things were working out rather well.

The fair was magic. Dad said they could stay as long as it took them to spend twenty pounds, which Alice thought would last forever but which actually disappeared in about an hour. They went on the ghost train, which wasn't even a bit scary, and on the Octopus, which was brilliant. They rode on the swingboats and the flying teacups, and Alice won two baby trolls by rolling balls into slots with numbers in and making them add up to twenty one. She let Dad have a go at rifle shooting and he won another baby troll. But the best thing was the big wheel. At first she hadn't thought she'd get her father to go on it. 'I'm scared!' he said. 'I want a hot dog!'

Alice counted the money that was left, and said he could have a hot dog, but only if he went on the big wheel with her.

'You're very cruel,' said Dad.

'You can have a hot dog with onions!' said Alice.

'I'll have to have tomato ketchup as well if I'm going on that thing,' said Dad, gazing up into the sky with a horrified expression on his face. 'It might be the last meal I ever eat!'

'Better go on the big wheel first in case you're sick,' said Alice, and they joined the queue. A couple of minutes later the wheel stopped and the fairground man began to load people on. When it was their turn he sat them down in a swingy seat and snapped a metal bar shut to hold them in.

'I want to go home!' squeaked Dad.

The fairground man winked and pulled a lever, and suddenly the wheel began to turn, carrying them up, up, up to the very top. They sat there, swinging gently, while more people got on at the bottom. Alice

could see all of Bristol over the tops of the trees. She was so excited she couldn't speak. She could hardly breathe. And then the ride started properly, and the wheel spun round and round, round and round, with the lights flashing and the music blaring out, and Alice wasn't stuck on the ground watching, she was in it, part of it, and she could see everything in the world. 'I can see London!' she screamed. Everyone was screaming. 'I can see Scotland, I can see my school, I can see Australia, I can see the moon!' She was on top of the world and she had broken a world record. It was her day, after all.

7

Recently Buried Chickens

They spent the last of the money on two hot dogs and wandered back to the car with the baby trolls. Alice was so happy she was half afraid she was dreaming, and in a moment she'd wake up to find herself at the back of a long, bad-tempered queue in Marks and Spencers. She decided to give one troll each to Oliver and Rosie because they hadn't been to the fair.

When they got back everyone was sitting watching television while dinner cooked in the oven. Oliver looked half asleep, which wasn't surprising, because going around the shops on a Saturday was just about the most tiring thing Alice could think of. Rosie and

Polly Penguin were perched on Grandpa
Fox's knee as usual.

And Mum was surrounded by the most
enormous pile of carrier bags. She had
bought a jumper for Alice and a dress for
Rosie and socks and a shirt for Oliver and
three pairs of shoes. She had bought a set
of pillow cases and two cushion covers,
three paperback books and a CD, and a
pair of black tights with sparkles on. She
had bought a bath sponge shaped like a
pineapple and a nail brush shaped like a
melon. They must have had to stand in a
dozen different queues.

'What, no soap shaped like a strawberry?'
said Dad. 'No duvet? No Second World War
air raid shelter? How are we ever going to
manage?'

Mum opened the last carrier and pulled
out a box of Dad's favourite chocolates.

'Now you're talking!' said Dad, tearing at
the wrapping.

'We're just about to have dinner!' said
Grandma Fox. Dad put the chocolates
down in a hurry.

Mum came over and gave Alice a hug. 'You're looking tired,' she said.

Alice didn't feel one bit tired, just dazed, but she wasn't going to say so because being tired was a thing that might make Mum and Dad decide to go home earlier. 'Never mind,' said Mum. 'After dinner Grandma Fox wants to have one quick game of chess with Oliver, and then we'll set off and you can have a nice sleep in the car.'

'I didn't know Grandma Fox could play chess!' said Alice.

'Of course she can,' said Mum. 'Who do you think taught me?'

They had chicken casserole and fresh fruit salad for dinner and then it was time for the chess game. Alice hoped Oliver wouldn't take too long to win. It was half past six already.

'You can put your baby troll on the table to be your lucky mascot if you like!' she said. She had seen people do this on television. Once she had seen someone bring along a cabbage to be their lucky mascot, and the quizmaster had smiled politely at the cabbage and said hello to it. Perhaps the troll would help Oliver to win more quickly, and then they could go home.

'Thank you, Alice,' said Oliver, who was looking a bit livelier since he'd had his dinner. He perched the baby troll on the table next to his new chess board, which was beautiful. The old set had nasty little plastic pieces and a flimsy board which folded down the middle and was all cracked and torn along the fold. *This* chess board was made of solid wood, and so were the pieces. It was a very fine chess set. If only you could do something interesting with it, like rolling balls at it and seeing how many pieces you could knock over! But chess wasn't like that at all. Oliver frowned, leaned forward and moved a white piece. The game had begun.

Alice watched for the first few minutes. Grandma Fox moved her black pieces quickly and calmly. She didn't look one bit worried about playing against Oliver. Alice remembered that Grandma Fox wasn't the sort of grandma who stayed at home all day looking after the house, like Alice's other grandma. Grandma Fox was a schoolteacher. She taught chemistry. She was probably quite clever.

Oliver was leaning further and further forward, his fists screwed up into clenched white balls and his knuckles digging into the sides of his head. His lips were tight and thin and his forehead one big frown. Alice had seen all this before. She looked round, and suddenly noticed that Rosie and Polly Penguin had disappeared. How long had they been gone? They could be anywhere. They could be doing anything. And if they'd done something bad, Mum was going to throw Polly Penguin in the bin. This was an emergency.

But Rosie and Polly Penguin were sitting halfway up the stairs, looking good as gold. In fact, Rosie had that specially good look that came over her when she had just emptied herself of badness by doing something really really wicked.

'Rosie,' said Alice, 'tell me what you've done. Quickly!' There might still be time to go and clear it up, while everyone was busy watching the chess game.

'Polly Penguin been good!' said Rosie.

Alice gave Rosie a long hard look.

'Are you *sure*?' she said.

'Good!' said Rosie, gazing up at Alice with huge brown innocent eyes. Alice sighed. She would have to check the whole house. She took Rosie and Polly Penguin with her, to keep an eye on them.

Alice, Rosie and Polly Penguin tiptoed in and out of every room in Grandma Fox's house while Alice checked for signs of mischief. They looked everywhere. Alice peered inside the toilet in search of furry mittens, and crouched down to look under Grandma Fox's bed. She turned all Grandma Fox's shoes upside down and shook them. She opened the oven and the washing machine and inspected the insides. She even poked her head round the back door to examine the garden for evidence of recently buried chickens.

There was nothing. Everything was as it should be.

'Polly Penguin been good!' said Rosie, again. Rosie had been following her around, her eyes huge with delight. Rosie thought it was a great joke. Alice didn't know what to make of it. Rosie had been perfectly good all day. Perhaps she had decided to have good days. This wasn't necessarily such a wonderful thing. If you *knew* she had been naughty, then you had to keep looking until you'd found what she'd done, but at least once you'd found it you could relax. If she *might* have been good, you didn't know if you could stop looking or not.

It seemed that life only ever got more and more complicated.

8

Checkmate

Alice took Rosie's hand and they went back
in to see if the chess game had finished.
Straightaway she could see that something
was wrong. The room was full of the most
silent silence she had ever heard. Oliver was
slumped forward, his hands covering his
face. The bits of face that showed between
his fingers were a dead grey colour. And, on
the chess board, there were more black
pieces than white. Alice counted, and
counted again. Grandma Fox had eight
pieces and Oliver only had six.

Oliver was going to lose.

Grandma Fox moved a black knight and
said: 'Check.' This was usually what Oliver

said, just before he won. When he won, he said, 'Checkmate.'

Oliver moved his white king.

Grandma Fox moved a black bishop and said: 'Check.'

Oliver banged his hand hard on the table. Mum and Dad looked at each other. Oliver moved his white king.

Grandma Fox moved the black knight again and said. 'Checkmate.'

For a moment the world stood still.

Then something terrible happened. All the frustrations of the day began to boil up inside Oliver like a fire of anger and misery. Losing the Alphabet Game to Alice and Alice getting the world record. Having to drag round the shops with Mum and Grandma Fox while Alice went to the fair. And now losing a game of chess to Grandma Fox with his entire family watching. Something in Oliver exploded.

'It's not fair!' he screamed, picking up the chess board and all the pieces and hurling them onto the floor. 'I hate you all!' Nothing was left on the table except the baby troll. Oliver grabbed it and threw it at Alice. 'You and your stupid lucky trolls!' he shouted. 'It made me lose! I never had a troll before and I never lost! It's all your fault!'

Alice managed to catch the troll. And then the room froze. Nobody moved. Nobody said a word. And the most dreadful silence of all was that of Grandma Fox. She gazed at Oliver as if she didn't recognise him. As if she had never really known him before.

Rosie was the first to move. She slipped down off Grandpa Fox's knee, from where she had been watching with her mouth wide open with astonishment, and set about picking the chess pieces up. 'Oliver been naughty!' she said, putting all the pieces back in their beautiful new wooden box. 'Oliver been naughty. Grandma Fox is the winner!'

And then Grandma Fox rose to her feet.

'Thank you, Roseanna,' she said. To Alice's amazement, she reached down and picked Rosie up. 'You have been a very good child today. I'm glad to see that you're growing up.' Rosie gazed proudly around the room as if to say: 'Well, look at this then!'

And then Grandma Fox turned to Oliver.

'I have never seen such disgraceful behaviour in my life,' she said. 'You clearly aren't old enough to have such a thing as a proper chess set. I have changed my mind. I will keep it here and use it myself.'

'No!' cried Oliver, and burst into floods of tears.

'I'm afraid so,' said Grandma Fox. She took the chess board and pieces and shut them up firmly in a cupboard. 'And you're to apologise to Alice.'

This was more than Oliver could bear and he ran out of the room.

'Oh, Oliver . . .' said Mum, and hurried off after him.

Alice sat quietly in the corner holding Oliver's troll. She felt all mixed up. She had wanted something bad to happen to Oliver, and it had – he had to go shopping instead of going to the fair. And that should have been an end to it. But now even worse things were happening to him, and Alice had had enough. This was *too much*. She wasn't enjoying it at all. From the hall came the sounds of Oliver crying and Mum making soothing noises.

'Well,' said Dad. 'I think we'd better be getting on home.'

The journey back was even worse than the journey there, because Oliver kept making little sniffy sobbing noises and nobody could make him stop until just after Reading, when, at last, he fell asleep. Rosie had already been sleeping for an hour. Alice sat in the dark as they sped along the motorway, trying to make sense of the day. Everyone had been the opposite of what they were usually. Rosie had been good. Oliver had been very very bad. And Alice, who never won anything, had become a world champion. It had all been very strange.

She looked down at her lap and the two baby trolls, her own and the one that had been Oliver's. She didn't know what to do with this troll now. Somehow she didn't really want it for herself. She turned round and put the troll at the back of the car with the road maps, where it could enjoy the view through the back window. She was still wondering what to do with it when she fell asleep.

9

P-Q

Rosie's troll, who was named Molly, went to live outside in Polly Penguin's shoe box, drowning in a thunderstorm a few weeks later.

Alice's troll, who was named Hideous, moved into the hutch with Aminal and the butterflies. Alice was secretly thinking of changing Aminal's name. Now that everyone in the family could say both *Aminal* and *Animal* (except for Oliver, who always called Aminal 'your guinea pig') there didn't seem any point to it any more, and she rather thought she might call him Alexander instead.

Polly Penguin continued to be almost

completely good. But then at Christmas Grandma Fox gave Rosie an adorable cuddly owl, called Ollie. Ollie Owl was by far the nicest present she had ever bought Rosie, but you only had to look into Ollie's eyes to know that she was not going to be a well-behaved sort of owl. There followed a most unfortunate accident involving the Christmas turkey, a tube of glue, a bottle of family-size baby shampoo, a packet of golden syrup flavour breakfast cereal and the microwave oven. Rosie, Polly and Ollie were all sent up to their rooms while everyone else tried to scrape the mess off the walls, but Christmas dinner was ruined and in the end they had to have frozen pizza.

Oliver was never quite the same again after the visit to Grandma Fox. For the next three days after the Worst Day of his Life, he hid away in his room. He barely spoke a word and he hardly ate a thing. When he eventually came out he seemed to have grown three inches taller. He wrote a long letter to Grandma Fox, and received a letter in return. Nobody ever knew what the letters said except for Grandma Fox and Oliver. When they next went down to visit, just before Christmas, Grandma Fox gave Oliver a hug as usual. But this time she gave almost exactly the same hugs to Alice and to Rosie. You could hardly tell the difference any more.

And, after lunch, to Alice's horror, Grandma Fox and Oliver played chess again. This time nobody wanted to watch. Grandpa and Rosie were busy tiling the bathroom. Dad was dozing in front of the television. And Mum was going into Bristol to do some last bits of Christmas shopping.

'I'll come with you!' said Alice.

'Shopping?' said Mum in amazement.

'Anything!' said Alice. Anything to get out of the house.

When they got back, with a total of eight carrier bags, Alice tiptoed inside very warily. But there were Oliver and Grandma Fox, sitting on the settee and talking quietly to each other.

'How did it go?' asked Mum.

'Oliver lost,' said Grandma Fox. 'But he lost gracefully this time, and he played a better game than before. One day he'll be beating me. But not for another five years!'

Oliver smiled sheepishly. And Grandma Fox let him have the beautiful chess set back, as his Christmas present. Rosie got Ollie Owl. And for Alice, there was a clay modelling set which you could use to make animals and jewellery and bake them hard in the oven.

It was a much better visit than the last one.

Oliver never played the Alphabet Game again. Alice asked him to play on the way down to Bristol, but he explained that he was feeling too carsick. She asked him to play on the way back, but he couldn't manage because his legs were aching so much.

And the troll that would have been Oliver's? She somehow stayed in the back of the car and became the Car Troll. She was named P-Q.

'P-Q?' said Dad, when he heard. 'Strange

sort of name, isn't it?'

'It's because she's a well-behaved troll and always minds her Ps and Qs,' said Alice, looking sideways at Oliver, who pretended not to hear. But this was not the real reason. Alice knew the real reason, and Oliver knew the real reason. The real reason was the sign that said:

**POSSIBLE
QUEUES
AHEAD**

It was still there on the motorway, and, every time they passed it, Alice would turn round, reach P-Q down from the back window and wave the troll's fat little arm gently at the sign. She would never forget the day she broke the World Record. And, for sure, neither would Oliver.

Read other stories about A L I C E

ALICE'S SHOOTING STAR

ALICE Singer
sometimes felt very
ordinary. Her brother
Oliver was a chess
champion, and her
sister Rosie was famous
for causing trouble and
telling enormous lies
about her schooldays, which were
filled with camel races and trips to the
moon. Mum and Dad were trying to train
her to tell the truth. Alice knew this was
a dangerous plan, but she couldn't have
guessed what havoc Rosie would create
at her Christmas play – or that it would
lead to Alice becoming the star of the
neighbourhood.

ALICE'S SHOOTING STAR
by TIM KENNEMORE

ISBN 1842702394   £4.99

Read other stories about A L I C E

ALICE'S BIRTHDAY PIG

ALICE'S birthday was approaching and the thing she wanted most in the world was a pig.

The thing she wanted second most was to learn to say the word 'animal' properly. It always came out as 'aminal', and Alice was tired of her brother Oliver teasing her about it. But her birthday present would change things forever . . .

'Acutely observed' SUNDAY TELEGRAPH

'Beautifully crafted story . . . funny and touching by turns' SCHOOL LIBRARIAN

ALICE'S BIRTHDAY PIG
by TIM KENNEMORE

ISBN 1842702408   £3.99